DEADLY BENEVOLENCE

DAWN BROWER

ACKNOWLEDGMENTS

First thank you to Victoria Miller for making me another wonderful cover — I love every one you have made for me. I look forward to what you create next. Keep being the brilliant person I know you are.

Also a big thanks to my beta readers Megan M and Jennifer U. You were my first test subjects and helped me to iron out some of the kinks. I hope you enjoy some of the changes I have made so far. Also hats off to my proofreader extraordinaire, Elizabeth E. Thanks for helping spot some of those typos we all missed and making this book shine brighter.

Lastly, but certainly not least, a huge thanks to Leona for pushing me to write a zombie short story. This was a fun challenge and one I hope worked out well.

Zombies? What's not to like? This story is unlike anything I've written or probably will ever write. When asked to write it I wondered if I could even give something of this nature justice. I'm a romance writer first, but I love all things that go bump in the night. In a nutshell…challenge accepted.

My son, Nathan helped me plan out the characters. Nathanial was named after him and although he absolutely abhors the nickname, Nat, he forgave me its use—but only this once. Nathan is the reason this book exists. After all he is the number one zombie lover in my family. Nathan—I hope you like it (even though you said everyone should have died at the end.) Oops… Spoiler alert…some people live.

If you are a zombie lover—read on. It's a quick and deadly ride.

PROLOGUE

The heat in the room suffocated him. They had raised the temperature in the room because they believed the disease didn't flourish in high heat.

They were wrong—it thrived on it. Multiplied and spread faster with each elevation. Before long, it would be everywhere, and no one would be safe. She'd made sure to explain it to him in lengthy detail—so he'd understand why they had a limited amount of time. Time was more important than ever—so many already dead—and it was running out.

He rose from his seat to leave the room. The stale air was getting harder to breathe in—combined with the stench of body odor and sweat—he was desperate to get some fresh air.

"Where are you going?" she asked.

"I can't take it any more..." He paused. "Do you need me to stay?"

For her, he'd endure. If she needed him to, he'd walk over hot coals.

She shook her head. "No, if you need some space get some. Come back soon though."

He nodded. "I will be back I promise."

He kept his promises.

Once he was in the hallway, he let the door click shut. Just being outside of the room helped. They were leaving soon. Escape had become a necessity. Everything was in place—planned in advance just for this possibility. They were supposed to be gone already, but disaster had struck.

Archibald Doll had contracted the disease.

Best laid plans—what was Murphy's Law? Anything that can happen would happen? Something like that anyway. That was what they were going through. With Archibald in the middle stages of the disease and no cure in sight, they'd be saying goodbye soon.

Her heart was breaking, and he couldn't do anything to stop it.

"Lieutenant Grean," a voice called.

He halted, turned, and addressed the speaker.

"Sir?"

"How is my father doing?"

As if he cared. Wilhelm didn't care about anyone. Who did the evil bastard think he was fooling? The man was counting down the minutes until Archibald died.

"He's failing."

He nodded. "Has Luciana made any progress on her cure?"

Ah, the root of his concern. He wanted the cure. Wilhelm could use it to gain ultimate control over the masses. Everyone wanted to get a hold of a cure. People were dropping like flies, only to raise right back up and destroy the ones they loved. Archibald would do the same.

He wouldn't let anyone destroy Lucy. Her grandfather's death would hurt, but she'd move forward. Her mission would keep her going.

"I think she's hit a wall."

"I see. Let me know if anything changes." He paused. "Tell her to come see me as soon as possible with an update."

She was never going to be within his reach again. They were leaving in a few short hours, after she said her final goodbyes. Maybe he should step things up a bit. Something in Wilhelm's eyes made him nervous. Did he know what they planned?

No Wilhelm couldn't. He'd been very careful.

"Lieutenant."

Why couldn't they leave him alone? Especially this dickwad. Hatred for the douche bag soared through his veins. The bastard had broken her heart.

"Captain," he replied, holding back his distaste.

"How is Archibald?"

"Fine." He grated his teeth together. It took an enormous amount of self control not to snarl at him. "Do you need anything else?"

He shook his head. "Do you think she'll leave his side soon?"

"I don't know—she's committed to seeing this through."

To prevent any further questioning he spun on his heels and headed in the opposite direction of the captain.

Being around him left a bad taste in his mouth. Soon, neither one of them would have to deal with anyone in Wilhelm's compound again. Archibald had made sure Luciana had choices. His granddaughter meant the world to him, and he'd wanted her safe from his deranged son.

It was highly possible Wilhelm had Archibald infected to get rid of him.

Maybe he shouldn't have left her alone. He doubled back to check on her. There were two soldiers now stationed outside the door. Since when did the room need to be guarded?

"What's going on?"

They saluted, and both guards failed to meet his gaze.

"Sir, we were ordered to watch over Dr. Doll."

He just bet they were...

"Right. Well, I'm back. You can be at ease. Go take a break."

They eased slightly, but neither one moved.

"Sir, we can't do that."

Just as he expected—Wilhelm knew. He had to act fast. They had run out of time.

"I see." He nodded. "You will understand why I have to object to that."

He jumped forward and knocked them both unconscious before they could react to his words. The door flew open, and Luciana poked her head out.

"What's going on?"

"We need to leave now." He gestured for her to come all the way out of the room. "Your father knows."

"But grandfather. . ." She chewed on her bottom lip.

"He's gone, Lucy. We can't save him."

"I know," she said, resigned. "I just hate leaving him.

He grabbed her hand and led her away from the room. They didn't have much time. If they didn't make their escape, there would be no way for them to be free. At least he'd made contingency plans. Everything they required to get away from her father's compound was secured in a nearby vehicle. They would be gone before Wilhelm could react.

Then Dr. Luciana Doll could work on her cure in peace, and in turn, save the world from her father's demented plans.

Jaesin Grean, or Sin as most people called him, took in the room and everything inside of it. Lucy hunched over her favorite apparatus, the microscope her grandfather gave her, didn't hear him enter. On a gurney, to her left, a woman in the last stages of the deadly disease struggled to get free from the restraints holding her down. Lucy ignored her too. She tended to have a one track mind as she studied for a cure to the disease running rampant in the war torn world they now lived in.

"Aren't you worried she'll get free?"

Lucy glanced up at him with dazed eyes. She shook her head, and a few strand of her midnight-black hair fell over her forehead. Without much care, she brushed the loose curls behind her ear. "No." She shook her head. "Why would I?"

Dr. Luciana Doll had been his best friend since they'd both turned four years old and attended the same nursery school. For the twenty-five years that followed, they proved to be damn near inseparable. Except for his stint in the military and his army ranger training, they'd always been in close contact with each other. Which proved to be useful when all hell broke loose. A version of cholera broke out destroying humankind as they knew it.

The strand, new and deadly in ways they never could have anticipated. It spread fast and wide. The disease started in Africa, and not long afterward, it went worldwide. Lucy believed she could find a cure. Sin held his opinion in. What he really believed didn't matter. Lucy wanted to find a cure—her soft heart would accept nothing less. Sin stood by her side and made sure nothing happened to her. No one and nothing mattered more to him than his best friend. If he lost Lucy—no it was best not think about what would happen to the world if that scenario became a reality.

Because Sin would destroy everything...

He studied the decaying flesh and held in a cringe. Sin didn't show weakness, and the sight was a little gruesome to take in. To the outside world, he couldn't care less. Well he didn't, not really. Disgust rolled through him in waves. He wouldn't mention the smell—he tried not to breathe in too much while in the lab. How Lucy put up with it for hours on end, he'd never understand. Seriously, if he had to find a comparison, it was the equivalent of putrid meat baking in the hot sun. The only thing missing was the buzzing flies...

"She appears a little more decomposed than the rest of them."

Lucy shot him a defeated glance and chewed on her

bottom lip. "I'm trying, Sin. I thought I found something—"

A sigh escaped his mouth before he could stop it. Damn it. He hated seeing her so crushed with the failure to find a cure. He'd take on the world for her, but this was her show. He had to let her find her own way.

He frowned. "But you were wrong."

She nodded. "Yes. I feel like I'm getting close, but no, I'm afraid it's a long way off."

The woman pulled on the gurney strings. Her grey decaying flesh ripped on the restraints. A few pieces of loosened flesh fell off and fluttered to the floor. Sin had to hold back another cringe. He didn't want to let her know how much it bothered him to be around the undead. They seriously grossed him out on levels he could never fully explain. The woman might have been beautiful once. Sin couldn't really see it now. Blonde stringy hair caked in dirt clung to her head, and what might have been high firm breasts, now nothing more than flat pancakes of rotted flesh.

"I'm sure you will figure it out."

Lucy ignored him and turned back to her microscope. "I've isolated a strain in the bacteria I think might be responsible for—"

"Turning people into zombies?" Sin finished her sentence for her. That happened when you spent a lot of time with someone—and also the only person you communicated with for months on end. People didn't just roam by these days. Strangers were always suspected of evil before anything else.

At least for Sin. He didn't dole out trust easily.

She glared at him and then crinkled her nose. "I don't like that word."

An old argument between them—Lucy didn't want to think of them for what they were—zombies. No matter how much she denied it, they were dead. At a certain point, there was no saving them from becoming mindless killers.

"I don't see why not? They are essentially dead."

"But they aren't, if I find a cure—"

"You might be able to save someone in the first stage of the disease. The ones this far along..." Sin shook his head. "They are not savable."

Lucy sighed. "I know. I wish I could, but they have deteriorated too much for me to do anything to help them. The only thing they are good for is to further my research. Perhaps their sacrifice will help others to beat this horrible disease."

"Just keep trying. It's all you can do."

Lucy turned back to her work. "I know." She leaned forward and studied the slide under the microscope.

This disease only became a part of their reality in the past two years. Lucy, being a child prodigy, graduated from medical school and had been working as a resident at the Mayo clinic. She'd been doing some ground breaking research into cures for cancer only switching gears when the cholera outbreak took root. Ever since her grandfather became ill, she'd been studying it and attempting to find a cure in her own underground laboratory. Her biggest regret centered on her grandfather. Lucy's inability to find a cure in time to save him nearly decimated her.

Sin glanced back over at the sick woman on the

gurney. His stomach flip flopped and churned at the sight of her. The strap holding her down snapped loose and she stretched her arms toward Lucy. Her bony fingers were inches away from reaching Lucy's white lab coat. Sin sighed, pulled his K-bar out, and walked over to her in two quick strides. Before she could harm Lucy, he pulled her hair back and plunged the blade into her skull. Her dull eyes blinked closed as her final death took root. Sin let her head fall down and plop onto the gurney.

Lucy glanced up startled. "What did you do?"

Sin stared into her eyes, completely unapologetic.

"She got loose. I did what I had to."

"Damn it!" Lucy threw the pen she'd been holding in her hand. It plopped on the silver counter and pinged across the polished finish. "I need them alive. Otherwise, they are no good to me."

Sin's mouth formed a firm hard line. "What would you rather I'd done? Let it maul you to death?"

"She."

"Excuse me?" Sin asked, baffled.

"That's a woman on that table."

"I know that." Of course he did. What was the big deal?

Lucy shook her head. "Do you? You said *it*."

He sighed. Did he say it? He very well could have. Sin didn't like to think of them as real people. "Doesn't matter. I couldn't let *her* harm you."

"I know." Lucy scrubbed her hands over her face. "I'm just a tad frustrated."

"I'm sure we can find another one for you to experiment with."

"It's so sick that we need to think this way. They are human beings, and we don't consider it wrong to gather one roaming around and poke and prod them."

"You're thinking about it too much, Doll." Sin pulled her into his arms. He wrapped them around her and did his best to comfort her. He hated seeing her so upset. "It'll be fine. Why don't you go get some rest? I can take care of disposing of her body."

He made sure to say *her* instead of *it*. Sin didn't need her berating him anymore about his lack of empathy to the infecteds status as former living people. As long as he and Lucy made it—nothing else mattered to him.

"Yeah you might want to take a shower yourself when you're done."

"Why?"

"You have some uh—grey matter splattered in your hair. Don't get me wrong, I kind of like the blond grunge look. It compliments your blue eyes rather well." Lucy grinned and shrugged, her elbows bent at her side with her hand held out. "If you want, you can keep sporting it. I can find a way to live with your new fashion sense."

Lucy's deep, throaty snicker filled his ears. A warm fuzziness spread through him to hear her so happy. If laughing at him helped her cope, he hoped she found a lot of stuff humorous about him. Still, she probably did have a point, killing them always did leave a mess. He'd no doubt get even messier while he disposed of the body too.

"Yeah, when I get back in, I'll make sure it's the first thing I do."

"I'm sorry I snapped at you." Lucy's emerald-green eyes filled with remorse. "I know you were only protecting me. Lord knows I wouldn't have survived this long without you. My father—"

"Will never find you. Don't worry. I made you a promise, and I intend to keep it."

Wilhelm Doll was a sadistic bastard and saw his daughter as his personal property. Sin would die before he let him get to Lucy.

"I believe you."

Lucy bit her lip as tears formed in the corner of her eyes. One fell down, leaving a trail of wetness on her porcelain-white skin. Sin wiped it away and kissed her forehead.

"Are you going to be okay while I take care of—" He glanced over at the woman's corpse again and sighed. "her..."

"Yes, of course, go do what you need to do."

"While I'm outside, I'll do a perimeter check too. It doesn't hurt to be too careful."

"You're right. You always are."

Sin smirked. "Of course I am."

Lucy laughed. "So humble too. What would I do without you?"

"You'll never have to know."

He'd make damn sure of it too.

"Grandfather said the same thing." Sadness filled Lucy's eyes.

Pain stabbed his chest. Archibald Doll had been an amazing man. If not for his foresight, they wouldn't have the means to survive in this new world. He'd built the secret underground compound they lived in, and only told his granddaughter about its location. He'd also stocked it up with enough supplies to last them for years.

"He couldn't help what happened to him. You know he'd be here if he could be."

Lucy took in a deep breath and exhaled with a large whoosh of air. "Yes, he would. He's the reason I keep moving forward and trying. I *will* find a way to cure everyone, if it's the last thing I do."

"Well, let's hope it doesn't come to that." Sin walked over to the dead woman and wrapped her in a sheet to dispose of her. He'd burn her once he got her outside. "Now go take a shower and a nap. You need to rest if you're going to find the answers you seek."

Lucy nodded. Her gaze softened as she studied him. "Thank you again, Sin."

"You don't need to keep thanking me. I wouldn't be here, either, if not for you."

It made him uncomfortable. He didn't need her gratitude. As long as she remained safe and happy, all was right in his world.

"I wouldn't want to spend the end of days with anyone else. You really are the best friend I could ever have."

"Count on it." He held her gaze, reassuring her.

Lucy's lips wobbled into a sad smile. "Keep me posted while you're outside. I'm not going to be able to sleep until I know you're safely back inside."

"Will do, Doll."

"That's an order, Sin."

Sin saluted her. "Yes, ma'am"

Lucy chuckled as she left the lab. Sin let his arm fall to his side as he resumed his task of removing the dead woman. Once he came back inside, he'd make sure Lucy got the sleep she needed. If he didn't keep tabs on her, she'd work for days without rest. With any luck, she'd be asleep, and he wouldn't have to strong arm her into taking care of herself.

He wouldn't hold his breath though. Sin knew her too well. Lucy took stubbornness to all time highs. It was best to deal with the situation and fast.

No time like the present to dispose of a rotted zombie…

2
____

S in carried the body down a long winding tunnel. Near the end, a wheel barrow leaned against the wall, awaiting its next use. It came in handy more often then he'd like. He tossed the sheet covered woman into its shallow depths and grabbed the handle easing it through the narrow passage way. The tunnel hit what appeared to be a dead end.

He eased the wheelbarrow down with a quiet thud to open the door to the outside, hidden behind some high tech gizmos Archibald Doll invented before his death. Sin activated the release, and it unlatched into darkness overhead, not much different than the one he exited. There appeared to be no movement around him. It gave him the opportunity to take a moment and breathe in some fresh air as he scanned the area for possible intruders.

When he saw no sign of anyone lurking around the perimeter of the entrance, he moved forward. He created a pit a half a mile through the lush green area of Prentice

Cooper State Forest for disposal of the dead. Archibald chose the area to build his underground compound because it happened to be near the Tennessee River and close enough to a town if necessary. Plus he'd thought no one would think to search in the deep recess of Tennessee to locate him or his granddaughter. Who hid out in the general area of a state forest?

Sin heard a twig snap. The sound echoed through the forest putting him on guard. He dropped the handle of the wheel barrow and knelt down, scanning the area. He flipped on some night vision goggles over his eyes and searched the trees for movement. Two figures headed in his general direction. He didn't know if they were the infected, or if they planned to gain access to Lucy. Either way he'd have to deal with them. The dead woman could wait. No chance of her getting up and walking away. The two approaching individuals, on the other hand, were an immediate concern.

Sin hid behind a tree and waited until they neared. Footsteps plodded on the moist ground. Once they passed him, he stepped forward, knocking one of them in the back of the head. He fell down quickly, plopping to the ground with a dull thump.

"What the hell—" The other man moved over to his friend's limp body.

Sin circled around him in complete silence until he reached forward and wrapped his arms around his neck. The man struggled against him jabbing his elbow into Sin's stomach. He grunted as pain shot through him, but refused to let go. The man pulled at his arm, his nails digging into his flesh, attempting to loosen Sin's hold. After several seconds passed by, he slumped forward to the cold ground. Both men were knocked unconscious. Sin had to act fast and get them both inside the compound. He needed to have them secured so he could interrogate them. First, he needed to dispose of the woman's body.

They should be out long enough for him to take care of it all.

Sin moved swiftly, first dumping the corpse into the pit and letting it fall down to the bottom. He reached into the pocket of his BDUs and pulled out some water resistant matches. The match flicked into a flame as he ran it across the coarse surface, and tossed it into the bottom of the pit already soaked with an accelerant. The fuel saturated earth lit up into a small bonfire, heat floating up, warming Sin and the cold air around him. The fire crackled as smoke rose from the pit, burning his nostrils.

Time to take care of the two intruders—the woman would be gone soon, consumed by the intensity of the heat. The charred scent already permeated the air around him as he left the zombie remains in the fire pit.

He rushed back to where the other two men were knocked out cold. When he reached the area he'd left them, he inhaled a shocked breath. Only one of the men still lay unconscious on the ground.

"Don't do anything stupid, and I won't have to harm you."

Fuck, one of them managed to wake up. He'd deal with it. Sin turned around and peeked over at the man standing to his left. He held a compact handgun pointed at Sin's head.

How to deal with the situation? The man held his weapon with experience, he probably had training. But

Sin didn't doubt his own skills, with the right approach he could disarm the man and regain control. Lull him into a sense of security and then hit him hard—distraction was Sin's best defense. Get the guy talking and divert his attention.

"Who are you?"

The man's stance remained steady. His gaze never left Sin. "Someone who needs your help."

"I don't believe you." No one who came searching for him actually wanted his help. They were usually sent by Lucy's father. The rat bastard thought he could force his daughter into compliance. He didn't know her well if he truly believed she'd give in willingly to his demands. Sin made her a promise, and he intended to keep it. These two were not going to take her back to her evil father.

The man sighed and put his gun into the holster at his side. He held up his hands and pleaded, "I'm telling you the truth. I—or rather Nat needs Lucy's help."

Sin had been right. He came searching for Lucy. Could he trust the man didn't mean her harm? No, he couldn't. Lucy's safety came first. It was best to continue with his plan to stall for time and distract him until he could knock him out again.

"Nat?"

"You know him. Captain Nathanial Tyger."

Damn it. He meant the gnat. His former—and very annoying—commanding officer, the one man guaranteed to get on his nerves just by breathing. It also told Sin all he needed to know about the man standing before him. His training was legit and probably as good as his had been.

"Then we have nothing to discuss. No way in hell am

I letting gnat anywhere near Lucy. I know he chose her father over her."

The man shook his head, desperation filled his voice. "Please. Let her be the one to decide. Nat needs her help. I know she's been working on a cure."

Sin's eyes shot upward, pinning him with a hard stare, the situation finally dawning on him. "So he has it then? He's dying?"

Dejected, he admitted, "Yes, it's in the first stage. She's his only hope."

Sin disagreed, "No, he has none. She can't do anything for him."

"You're lying. Let me talk to her."

The man didn't appear to want to take no for an answer. Too damn bad. Sin didn't care if the gnat died— but Lucy might. He weighed his options. Should he let her know and make a decision for herself? She might not forgive him if he left them out here and ultimately signed the gnat's death warrant. He needed all the information before he could make a decision.

"Who are you, and why do you care?"

"I'm Deyn." He pointed to Nat. "His older brother."

News to him...

"Gnat never mentioned having a brother."

"Because we're half brothers. We didn't grow up together. He didn't know I existed until a couple years ago. Our father did his best to keep us ignorant of each other."

Sin still didn't want to allow them inside. It went against his better judgment to allow anyone inside the compound—especially these two. It was supposed to be a haven for Lucy. The two men before him disrupted it, creating chaos in their relatively peaceful existence.

"Give me one good reason to help you. Hell, better yet, give me one fucking reason to believe all this bull shit."

Deyn hesitated and studied Sin. The gnat's brother better start talking or Sin would make sure he stopped for good. He lacked patience, and what little he had was running on empty.

"If not for us, Lucy's father would already be here. She'd be back with him, and she'd have no choice but to do what he wanted."

"Lucy would never do what he wanted."

"No?" He raised one of his eyebrows. "Even if it meant saving you?"

Damn it. The bastard had a point. Lucy would do anything to save him.

"How do I know you're not lying? Buying time for him to get here?"

Deyn's lips twitched into a smirk clearly outlined by the moonlight streaming over his face. "You don't. I *can* guarantee you won't make it without our help. We know what his plans are."

Of course they did... Decision time had arrived, and Sin didn't like any of the choices.

If only the zombies were the ones they needed to worry about. The walking corpses were far easier to deal with. Wilhelm Doll threatened the world in a different way. He planned to use the spreading disease to conquer the world. World domination and control over its population—it drove the man in a powerful way. Lucy had the misfortune of being the key to him gaining it all. Being so close to finding a cure made her desirable in ways she'd never been before. If Wilhelm controlled the cure, he could also pass it out to only those completely loyal to him. Sin needed to know Wilhelm's next move. It wouldn't do any good to mull over everything. Deyn and Nat had information he needed. If it became necessary he could always kill them both later. Decision made. Sin nodded at Deyn.

"Pick him up. You can either carry him or toss him in the cart over there. Follow me."

Sin didn't stop to see if he actually did as he ordered. He just kept walking. If he really wanted to see Lucy, he'd do as Sin instructed. He could hear the wheelbarrow behind him. So Deyn had decided his brother would be too heavy to carry. Sin didn't blame him there. He'd have done the same thing.

Sin activated the door with a remote he carried in his pocket. It slid open, and he eased inside. Deyn entered behind him pushing the gnat in the wheel barrow.

"Are we taking him all the way inside in the cart?"

He could give him an easy out and say yes, but Sin had a cruel streak. Besides, he liked knowing where he left the wheelbarrow. Made that part of his life a tiny bit easier.

"No. From here on, you need to carry him."

Deyn grunted his agreement and picked up his brother, tossing his limp body over his shoulder. "I'm ready. Lead the way."

Sin didn't acknowledge him. He just started to move down the winding hallway. When they reached a lighted area, he turned toward a small medical wing. He pointed to a small cot, and Deyn set his brother down on it.

"Where's Lucy?"

"Resting. When she wakes up, we can tell her what's going on with him."

Sin refused to say his name. He hated the man. If Lucy decided to help gnat and Deyn, he'd allow them to stay. If not—well he'd have no problem tossing them back outside again.

Deyn sat down on one of the beds. "Fine. I could use some rest. Wake us up when she's ready to talk."

Sin spun on his heels and exited the room. He clicked a lock on the door so they couldn't get out and cause trouble. Sin may have allowed them inside, but he still didn't trust them. He wanted a shower and some rest too, but first he needed to do a security check. Afterward, he'd get some shut-eye. His mind would be mush without proper rest, and he refused to allow anything to happen to his best friend. Her father would not get to her today or any day.

3

____

"Sin?"

He opened his eyes and blinked them back closed as bright light hit his pupils. "Lucy, what time is it?"

He peeked at her through tiny slits—the harsh light too much for his eyes.

"It's early morning... Just after five." She chewed nervously on her bottom lip. What had her so worried?

Sin rubbed his palms over his sleep deprived eyes, wiping the grit away. "Right. I think I've managed a few hours of sleep. Do you need something?"

Lucy punched his shoulder. Pain shot through it and spread throughout his already aching muscles. "You didn't let me know you made it back inside. It worried me when I woke up."

Oh yeah, he'd forgotten in all the evening's excitement...

"Couldn't have worried you too much." Sin sat up

and stretched his aching muscles. "You did manage to fall asleep after all."

"Don't be an ass. Sometimes you have no control over your body's functions. I'd exhausted myself." Lucy crossed her arms over her chest and pouted. "You were the first thing I thought of when I opened my eyes. That has to count for something."

Sin couldn't help teasing her. It kept them from falling into a pit of despair. Anything to bring some laughter into their lives would only be for the greater good. He also made it a habit to never lie to her. She needed to know about Nat and Deyn. "I know. I do have something to tell you."

"What?" She raised an eyebrow.

"I did run into a bit of trouble while disposing of the body."

"Really? Explain yourself." Her voice full of worry once again. She nibbled away at her bruised bottom lip.

Damn he hated distressing her. It was about to get a lot worse too.

"We have guests..."

Lucy bolted from the bed a whoosh of air expelled from mouth as she gasped for air. Her hands flew to her throat as she began to hyperventilate in front of him. Sin cursed as he hopped up and pulled her into his arms.

"Easy now. I handled it. You have nothing to worry about."

Damn him for blurting out the information. Of course she would overreact to the news. Someone, or more importantly, two someone's now invaded their safe haven. He should have handled the news better. Her breathing tapered off into a nice even patter. One breath in, one out, as he could feel her heart beat become steadier beneath the palm of his hand.

"Who are they? Did my father send them?"

He sliced his head left in a quick motion. "No. I don't think Wilhelm had anything to do with sending them. At least not directly."

Lucy pushed back on his chest and took a step back. She tilted her face upward and searched his eyes with her own. "Who are they?"

Sin took a deep breath and prepared to tell her who'd come to find them. "Nat is here along with his brother Deyn"

Lucy backed farther away from him, shaking her head in rapid angry jerks with each step she took. "Nat's here? No, you said my father had nothing to do with them being here."

"No, I said he didn't directly send them. I do think he drove them here in the figurative sense." Sin took a step forward trying to reach out to her, offering some sort of reassurance. He hated seeing her in pain. If he could, he'd take it away. If only her bastard father would just leave her alone. Maybe then they'd be able to have some kind of peace.

Fat chance in hell of that happening—Wilhelm would see them both dead first.

"I don't understand."

Sin took a deep breath and prepared to disperse the bad news.

"Nat's sick."

He could see when the news sank in. Lucy's mouth fell open and her emerald eyes widened in disbelief. Her fingers raked through her ebony locks. "No, not Nat..."

"Deyn thinks you can help him."

"What? No—I..." She paused, tilted her head and studied Sin. "I did complete a vaccine. It won't do any good to help him. It hasn't been tested, but perhaps this Deyn would be willing to try it out if I can save Nat." She paused again as she appeared deep in thought. "His brother you said? I don't recall Nat ever mentioning him."

Exactly what he'd said...

"Probably because they didn't meet until you and Nat parted ways."

"Ah, I see." Lucy began to chew on one of her finger nails. "What stage is Nat in?"

"Far as I can tell, it's still first stage, but I don't know how long he's been infected or the circumstances around how he came to be here yet." Sin considered his next words and decided to get them out, even if she ignored his advice. "I don't think you should see him."

He knew he didn't have a chance in hell of convincing her to abandon them. Sin knew her too well. Nat and Lucy carried something between them—a history she couldn't deny. Lucy would keep them both here. The research possibilities alone would be too tempting for her to resist. Nat and Deyn were there to stay—at least until they no longer proved useful.

"No, I want them here. I think this is the chance I've been waiting for. I haven't experimented with anyone in the first stages before. I will need some of his blood for testing." Lucy grabbed his arm. "Take me to them. I need more information. If it goes well and I act fast, maybe, just maybe, I might be able to help him."

"Don't make promises you can't keep."

"I'm not. I won't tell him anything other than I'll try. I would never give anyone false hope. How could you think I would?"

He did know that, but he also knew how she once believed Nat could be the man she'd spend the rest of her life with. Sin knew firsthand how she fell apart when she realized it would never happen. Nat broke Lucy's heart. If Sin got his wish, he'd see him dead for that alone.

"I don't. Not really. I just wanted to give you a fair warning to use caution as you speak to them."

Lucy nodded. "You're right. I don't want to make them believe in me—I've been working on this for a long time now. It's seems so futile. I'm close though. If the vaccine works...you know what it could mean right?"

He saw hope flood her face. Her brilliance shining through the green depths—Sin wanted this all to work for her. He did. The fear filling him to the brink rocked him onto his haunches. Not for himself—but for her. What this failure might do to her. She'd been devastated before. If she lost Nat... That could destroy her soul.

"I'm glad you've managed to get somewhere with your research. For your sake, I hope it works out. With the vaccine and with Nat, even if the ass doesn't deserve it."

Lucy chewed on her lip again. A bad habit she failed to break. Worry filled her eyes as she glanced at him. "Is he really sick? I mean, I know he's sick, you said he is, but is he, you know, *really* sick?"

She sought some kind of reassurance. Sin wanted to take away all her pain. He always had. This was beyond the realm of his capabilities.

"Do you mean is he delirious and unaware of his surroundings?"

"Yes."

Sin shook his head. "I'm not sure how far along he is. I haven't spoken to him. I kind of um—knocked him out before giving him a chance to speak. I should mention he happened to be walking when I smacked him on the head. That's a good sign right?"

"Yes, indeed it is." She nodded. "It makes me believe he hasn't been sick long. Good, it gives us a starting point. I'll know more after I speak to him." She walked toward the doorway. Lucy paused at the entrance and turned toward Sin. "Where can I find them?"

Sin scratched his head and began to fidget in front of her. "Yeah, I left them both resting in a locked room. I didn't want them roaming around the compound unguarded. They're probably still asleep."

"Too bad, it's time to wake up and get working. Time is not on our side with this one. We can't afford to waste it. Show me where you stashed them."

"Fine, I will show you where they are. You do have a point."

Sin brushed past her and exited his sleeping quarters. Nat and Deyn were about to be woken up—whether they liked it or not. When Lucy got an idea in her head nothing on Earth would stop her. The fact that she trailed closely behind him showed how determined she could be. He didn't see any reason not to give her what she wanted. Besides, the sooner she realized Nat couldn't be saved, the quicker he could kick them out of their sanctuary.

4

———

Sin led Lucy to the medical room he'd stuffed Deyn and Nat into. She pushed past him and unlocked the door using her palm to activate the panel. Once inside she scanned the room ignoring Sin. He should be irritated, but Sin could never be mad at her. As soon as she spotted Nat she rushed over to his side. Her hand flew to his forehead, the back of it resting against his pale skin.

"He's warm. How long has he been sick?" She directed her question at Deyn who'd sat up in his bed upon their arrival.

"Two days. As soon as your father injected it in him, we set out to find you. Well, first we destroyed all the intel he'd gathered on your location. We couldn't have him finding you first."

"What? He knows where we are?" Lucy's face became a shade of white almost translucent. Truly frightening to behold—she needed some color back on her pale skin. "How much time do we have until he finds us?"

Deyn stood up and walked toward them. A mulish expression filled his face as he stared at Lucy. "I told you we destroyed any information he'd accumulated on your whereabouts."

Lucy shot her gaze at Sin. "Do you trust him?"

He folded his arms across his chest, his legs spread enough to have equal balance, and glared at Deyn—distrust shooting out of his eyes.

"Not on your life. After you get what you need to help Nat, I'll start working on our security."

She nodded and turned her attention back to Deyn. "You said my father injected him. Why?"

"Nat started to—" He paused, glanced back at his brother. Worry etched across his face as he stared at Nat. Deyn turned back to Lucy, his eyes filled with pain. He shook his head and his eyes cleared—no emotions showing once again. All business, he continued, "How do I put this? He'd begun to question your father's methods. Wilhelm doesn't allow anyone to place doubt in his command. He used Nat as an example of what not to do. No one is willing to step up when they could be the next recipient of a dose of death."

Lucy's mouth fell open as shock spread across her features. This was not something either one of them expected to hear. Nat had been firmly in Wilhelm's camp when they escaped. It was the very reason their relationship fell apart.

"I don't believe you. When I left, Nat believed in my father's way of doing things. He wouldn't have doubts now."

"He wouldn't? Are you sure about that?" Deyn raised his eyebrows, mocking her. "You've kept in contact with him then. Know what's been going through his mind since you disappeared."

Lucy fidgeted and glanced everywhere but directly at Deyn or Nat. Sin wanted to punch the dickhead in the nose. How dare he upset her? His feet started to move before his brain caught up to his body's movements. He was almost to his side and ready to launch his fist.

Lucy held up her hand stopping him from acting.

Her silent disapproval caused him to stop in his tracks. She didn't want him to harm them. For her, he'd restrain himself, but if she got upset again, there would be no holds barred. He'd beat them bloody.

She turned her attention back to Deyn, this time staring him right in the eyes. "Don't be silly. Of course I haven't contacted him. We're supposed to be in isolation here. Which is why I don't know how my father could have located us."

Deyn snickered and rolled his eyes.

"You underestimate your father's abilities. He's been hunting you since you left. Once he has something set in his mind, he doesn't give up on it." Deyn turned to Sin. "You know I'm right don't you. It's why your hankering to go check the security you have in place."

Sin nodded. "I know."

"We don't have any time to lose. If you have a contingency plan, we need to act on it."

"How long do you think we have until Wilhelm comes searching for her?" Sin asked.

"You mean how much time did we buy you?" Deyn

asked, raising an eyebrow—reminding him what they claimed to do for Lucy already.

"Yes." Sin nodded, wanting more than ever to break his nose. He was starting to see the family resemblance.

"What are you two talking about?" Lucy demanded.

A shit storm was about to fall on them. He turned to her and said the words guaranteed to send fear coursing through her veins. "Your father is heading this way, Doll. We need to move."

She scrunched her brows together and pursed her lips. Slowly, she shook her head denying his words. Her head jerked up, her gaze landing on Nat's face. Lucy's chin jutted out in defiance and she turned her eyes toward Sin.

"No, we can't move yet," she said, shaking her head firmly. "I'm so close, and I can't help Nat if we relocate. I'll lose all of my research."

This was something Sin feared might happen—Lucy's stubborn streak coming out to play at the worst time possible—now he would have to plan for all possibilities. He studied Lucy and focused on her. Then he tilted his head toward Deyn and replied, "Which is why I'm asking him how much time he thinks we have."

"A week—two if we're lucky."

Sin nodded. "You have a week, Doll. Do you think you can work a miracle in that time?"

Lucy bit her lip, uncertainty filling her eyes. "I don't know..."

"What do you need from me?" Deyn asked, inserting himself into the conversation. "I'll do anything if it will help my brother."

Lucy turned her attention on him. Sin could see a

gleam of excitement take over her face. She'd been hoping he'd agree to be a guinea pig in her experiments —it appeared like she might get her wish.

"I have a vaccine—but it hasn't been tested."

Deyn remained quiet for several seconds, appearing to consider Lucy's words. His face remained impassive. Sin couldn't tell which way he'd lean, but he guessed he'd do it. The man seemed to care for his brother and he's indicated he'd do anything to save him. The supposition proved correct with his next question.

"Will it help Nat?"

"No, someone already infected..." Her lips scrunched up as she searched for the right way to explain the issue. She sighed, but still took a few moments before she continued. Lucy stared him in the eyes and elucidated, "It would only escalate the disease, but someone uninfected, it well, it could prevent them from ever getting the disease at best. At worst, it would build up in their immune system so they could fight it off if they ever got it."

"What are you not telling me?" Deyn asked.

Lucy twisted her fingers together to control her agitation. "As I said, it hasn't been tested. I have no idea what the possible side effects could be."

"You're reluctant to try it on someone." Deyn's lips formed into a grim line as he nodded his head at her. He made a quick decision and commanded, "You can test it on me."

"I didn't even ask..."

"But you wanted to." His grey eyes cold as steel. Sin could come to respect the man. He could relate to his loyalty—even if he didn't agree with it.

"Don't argue with him, Lucy. He's giving you what you want." Sin walked over and placed his hand on her shoulder, urging her to see reason. "You said you'd need Nat's blood. I'll go get some supplies out of the cabinet."

Sin left Lucy with Nat and Deyn as he crossed the room to gather the items she needed. He opened the cabinet and pulled out some alcohol pads, rubber gloves, a few syringes, and vials to collect her samples in. He put them all on a tray and carried them over to her. Lucy took them out of his hands and placed them on the bed beside Nat.

"I am just going to take a few vials of his blood so I can continue working on the cure." Lucy explained to Deyn. "There has been a key component missing in everything I've created up to this point. I'm hoping the answer is in Nat's blood."

She pulled on some gloves and then prepped Nat to take some of his blood. The needle eased into his vein, and Lucy pushed one of the vials into the syringe. Dark red blood began to fill the vial. Lucy repeated the action several times until she'd filled them all and placed them into the awaiting storage container.

"How is Nat's blood going to help?" Deyn asked.

Lucy pulled off one glove and shoved it into her glove covered palm, rolling them together as she peeled it off. She tossed them onto the tray and gave her attention once again to Deyn.

"I have only gotten the opportunity to study the infected in the later stages of the disease." She gestured toward his brother with a tilt of her head. "Nat is my first opportunity to study it before it takes root and destroys brain function. If the key is here...I'll be able to save him. If not, there's nothing I can do."

Deyn studied Nat, remaining quiet for several seconds. Sin believed he was worried, but it was hard to tell. His features remained unreadable. His gaze shifted upward and focused on Lucy.

"And when are you going to give me the vaccine?"

"Later today. I want to start working on the tests right now while the blood is fresh. I will come back in a few hours and check on Nat. I will bring the vaccine then."

"Fine. You really think there's a chance to save him?" Deyn stared down again at his brother. His gaze flew to Lucy's—emotions filling them again. He seemed to be having trouble bottling them up. "When Wilhelm injected him, Nat insisted I bring him to you. He swore you were his only chance. He has such faith in you."

Lucy's compassion blasted them all. Sin often wished she wasn't so soft hearted—at the same time he was thankful for it. If not for their friendship, he'd have turned into a monster. She kept him rooted.

"I can't make you any promises. I can only do my best. Now if you'll excuse me, I have some work to do."

Lucy left the room. Sin watched her go and turned his attention back to Deyn. "You will *not* hold her accountable if she doesn't succeed."

"Of course not." Deyn agreed. "I wouldn't. I just needed something—a little hope never hurts."

What a moron. Hope had the capability of hurting more than a knife twisting deep in a person's gut. When it failed to meet expectations, it jabbed you where you hurt the most—deep in your life force. It could leave you hollow and bitter. No, hope was for fools or the compassionate. Sin was neither.

"Except when she falls short at finding the cure. That hope will crash through you like an erupting volcano. I won't have you destroy her as it overflows." Sin crossed his arms and glared at him. "Now tell me exactly what happened so I can start preparing our departure."

Deyn nodded, but ignored his warning. Instead, he gave him a bit of information guaranteed to put him on high alert. "Wilhelm has created an army."

"Tell me something I don't know." Sin rolled his eyes.

"A zombie army."

Right—that was a different story and a confounding one too.

"Say that again?" Sin had to have heard him wrong. "How did he get the infected to enlist?" He stopped short of snorting at the ridiculousness of a zombie army.

"He's developed a device to control them. It's some kind of electrode. It attaches to their head." Sin just raised an eyebrow in disbelief, but nodded for him to continue. Deyn explained further, "He controls them from a remote location. It's kind of like having live zombie robots. Wilhelm pushes a button, and they get to work destroying everything in their path."

Shit storm? Try a nuclear cyclone about to descend on them at any moment—annihilation guaranteed.

"Nooo..."

The horror of what Deyn described—he couldn't even begin to picture it. A mob of zombies controlled by a power hungry monster; what a fucking mess. Sin thought it couldn't get any worse. He'd been wrong. The infected were cannon fodder, something he could use and not really worry about losing. Not that Wilhelm cared if anyone died.

Deyn frowned. "I'm afraid so. It's what got Nat into this mess. He started to question the man's methods. You don't do that and survive."

"Fuck. Do me a favor and don't tell Lucy this yet. I have to find a way to soften the blow first." He scrubbed his hands over his face. How was he to explain to Lucy how mad her father had become? She'd hoped to save the world—her father wanted to conquer it. Lucy knew her father was evil incarnate, but this would still be a blow to her.

Deyn nodded his head. "I can do that. I don't want her distracted anyway. If she knew everything her father did—she'd never be able to sleep at night."

"She barely does now. Trust me, she is well aware of what a malicious man Wilhelm Doll is. She has no illusions he will ever change." Sin paused and considered his next words. "Nat meant—still means something to her. She's putting on a brave face, but I know her. Lucy's blaming herself for his predicament. I don't want to add to her perceived guilt."

"She won't hear anything from me. When Nat wakes up, I'll tell him to keep his mouth shut."

Sin snorted. "Good luck with getting him to comply. Gnat never did follow orders. He sure didn't have any problem issuing them though."

He was an annoying bug. All Sin wanted to do was crush him between his fingers—or swat him out of existence. The only thing keeping him in check was he knew how much Lucy cared for him.

"Do you need any help? Preparing to leave that is."

Sin shook his head. "Not right now. When it gets closer to departure though, I will. Lucy isn't going to want to leave any sooner than necessary. I want to leave on a moment's notice."

Deyn nodded and then added, "He's going to attack with the zombie's first."

"Of course he is." Sin agreed. "He'd never put himself in any danger. He'll know I'd sacrifice myself before letting Lucy be harmed. I'd be willing to bet he let you two go knowing you'd head straight for her. He's hoping to kill us all off and grab Lucy."

"I wish I'd never let Nat talk me into trusting him. I didn't like him from the start, but I wanted to get to know my brother."

What a useless emotion. It was better to move forward. Looking backward was never a good idea. Regrets should remain where they were meant to be—firmly in the past. Sin didn't believe in them and wasn't going to let Deyn's bleed into the present.

"Having regrets now won't help any of us."

"I don't regret anything. Getting to know Nat—let's just say I'd do it again just for him."

Good. They were on the same page—hell looked like they were even reading the same bloody book. Deyn seemed like good peeps—but trust—would never come easy for Sin. He didn't like relying on people. In this case, he'd concede Deyn wanted to save Nat as much as Sin wanted to take care of Lucy. In that, they could become a team to survive the upcoming massacre.

"Understood. I'll leave you two be for now. I won't lock you in this time, but if I catch you doing anything you're not supposed to..." Sin paused and shot him an evil grin. "I'll shoot first and ask questions later."

"I get it. I know Lucy is your first priority."

Sin nodded at him and walked out of the room. He'd trust him for now—well as much as Sin trusted anyone—which was next to nil. Deyn didn't seem like he wanted to do them harm. Sin's trust only went so far. He stopped by the panel outside of the room and turned the security on to full alert. It would record all movement in the compound. If Deyn did do something out of the ordinary, the computer would pick up on it. Then he'd get a taste of Sin's lack of patience. He didn't deal well with betrayal and Deyn would feel every inch of his wrath. As soon as he could though, he'd put a bullet through Wilhelm's head. As long as that man managed to draw breath, Lucy would never be safe. If he could have one wish it would be for her to be settled, safe, and happy.

5

———

Sin did a quick perimeter check to reassure himself. He didn't want to leave anything to surprise him. Once he finished his task he went back inside and locked down the compound. No one could get in or out without his permission. He needed to check on Lucy's progress and get a better idea of how much time she required to make her possible cure for the gnat.

He found her hunched over her favorite spot staring into a microscope. She stood up and pulled the slide out and put another one in its place. Lucy placed her eye on the lens again and studied the results. She lifted her head and jotted a few notes on the paper sitting by her side.

"You have a minute?" he asked.

"Not really. I don't have a lot of time to get this done." She let out a deep breath and sighed. "It's a herculean task, Sin. I don't know if I'm up to it."

"Of course you are. I have faith in you." If anyone could pull a cure off in the zero hour, it was Lucy.

With a wobbly smile, she nodded. "I can always count on you to keep pushing me. I hope I'm up to your belief in me."

As if he'd ever give up on her...

"You've always exceeded every expectation set for you. Now is not the time to start doubting yourself." He pulled her forward and wrapped his arms around her. A hug would go a long way to making her feel better—and Sin always gave Lucy what she needed. "You've got this, Doll. Don't doubt yourself."

Lucy stepped out of his arms and stared into his eyes. "Thank you. I needed that."

"I know." Sin grinned. "Now I don't want to put you on the spot, but I need to have some idea on how long this might take you."

"I don't know..." She chewed on her bottom lip and stared at her microscope. "There's just so much to do and understand."

"I'm not asking for a definitive answer, just a ball park range of time."

"I can't give it to you." Her chin jutted out as her stubbornness came in full throttle.

"Not even an educated guess?" he asked, pushing her to give him an answer.

Lucy shook her head. "This is new territory to me—you need to plan our escape don't you?"

"Yes," he said. "We can't stay here. They gave us a week at best. I want to be gone before then. If they say a week, in reality, I'd give us three days."

"I just don't know if I can do it in that short of time." Lucy's gaze wandered to her microscope again. "I'll try though. Nat's life depends on my ability to focus."

"Have you made any progress?"

"Actually I have. I've added some components to Nat's blood. So far the white cells present seem to be working with it to attack the bacteria. It's amazing really." Her gaze wandered off. Sin was used to it happening though. When she became deep in thought or her brain latched on to an idea, she lost focus on everything but her new idea. He snapped his fingers gaining her attention.

"Does this mean you may have something to work with?"

Lucy nodded. "It is only one aspect of the serum I've been working on, but the short answer is yes. I need to run a few more tests. If it goes as I think it will, I might have an answer for you sometime tomorrow."

Sin nodded. "Good. That means we could leave sooner than I want to."

"I don't want to rush," Lucy reminded him.

"If I could help it, you'd have all the time you need. Unfortunately, this really isn't in my control."

Sin couldn't afford to give her more than three days to work on a cure. If her father got a hold of her—it wouldn't just be the end of her life. It would have a major impact on the world. The madman would unleash horrifying havoc on those still uninfected. He'd already begun his reign of terror, and now he managed to even corral the infected to his benefit. Once Lucy knew about his diabolical scheme to control the zombie population— she'd be even more appalled than him.

Lucy sighed. "I want to go check on Nat and give Deyn the vaccine. Will you come with me?"

"Of course."

"All right, let me grab the vaccine and then we can go to their room." She strolled over to a refrigerated storage unit and pulled out a vial and put it in her lab coat pocket. "Are they still locked inside the room?"

"No I left it unlocked and upped the security to monitor all movement. I wanted to give them the illusion of freedom."

Lucy studied him. "You're testing them"

"I am. If they're lying, we'll know soon enough."

Part of him wished they were. It would give him something to—pound on.

"I doubt Nat is faking being infected."

"No, on that one point, I agree with you. He is definitely sick. Deyn's motives are unclear to me." He respected the man, or rather his skills—but he was still unfamiliar. "Yes, I can see how he might want to protect and save his brother, but until I know for sure, he is an unknown quantity."

"I see. Let's go see what they are up to." Lucy exited the room.

Sin followed close behind her, watching everything as they made their way to the room Nat and Deyn occupied. When they reached the entrance, Lucy pushed open the door and walked inside. Nat sat up his head resting on the wall behind him, his eyes closed and his skin a shade lighter than when they saw him earlier. Nat's cheeks held some color, a slight pink, indicating his high fever. Sweat dripped down his forehead, and his coffee-brown hair was soaked from the accumulation. Deyn paced the room and ran his hands through his dark brown hair leaving it disheveled.

Lucy ignored Deyn and marched over to Nat's

bedside. His eyes shot upward at her approach. A smile formed on his face when he realized who came near. "Hey, Luce. It's good to see you."

Lucy snorted. "Don't flash those baby blues at me and think you're going to charm me. I'm immune now."

Nat's smile dropped from his face. Dejection shot out of those baby blue eyes Lucy referred to. "I'm sure you are. Still, I've never been so glad to see someone. Do you have any news?"

Lucy shook her head. "No. I'm sorry I don't have anything specific to tell you. I just came to check on you and vaccinate Deyn."

"Yeah, he mentioned you'd created a vaccine. Your father isn't going to like that. He'd rather dole out a cure to those worthy enough to get it. A vaccine is going to piss him off." He tilted his head in thought. "Although he'd find a way to use that to his advantage too."

"I'm well aware of what my father is capable of. I'm only disappointed it took you this long and being infected to finally realize it." Her tone filled with disappointment.

Sin forced himself to hide the smile fighting to form on his face. Good for Lucy. She should give the gnat hell. He'd made the wrong choice, and now no matter how many *I'm sorry's* he dealt out, she'd be unlikely to forgive him.

Lucy turned her back to Nat and went over to Deyn's side. Sin couldn't hear what she said, but he figured it had something to do with the vaccine. She gestured for him to go sit on one of the beds. He walked over to Sin and Nat and sat down on his own bed. Lucy went to the cabinets to gather supplies.

Nat glanced over at him. "I'm betting you're enjoying this."

"What?" he asked the epitome of innocence on his face.

"Lucy hates me now. You never did like me."

Sin smirked. "What I think of you has never been an issue. You fucked up all on your own. Lucy's very capable of making up her own mind about a person."

"I'm aware." He tilted his head. "But I also know you've made it perfectly clear you never thought I would be good enough for her."

"Thanks for proving me right. Made things so much easier for her to dump your sorry ass." He nodded toward Lucy. "Now if you could just do me a solid and die, we'd be good."

"God, you're a prick."

Unfazed, Sin let the insult roll off and said, "Thanks. I do try."

"Will you two stop it. Lucy will be back over here in a minute. This conversation will upset her. We need her focused not pissed off." Deyn glared at them.

"As much as I hate to admit it, he's right. She'd be ticked off at both of us. I'd rather her just stay mad at the gnat."

Nat rolled his eyes. "I'm not dying just to help you out."

"I know. Wouldn't expect anything less from you. You've always been a pain in my backside."

Lucy picked up a tray and carried it over to where Sin stood. Her eyes roamed across all of them and stopped to stare into his. "What are you three talking about?"

Nat, attempting to be a peacekeeper, played it off as nothing. "Making sure you stay stress free so you can concentrate on finding a cure sooner rather than later. I don't particularly want to die or become a mindless zombie"

Lucy scrunched up her nose. "I really do hate that word."

"What word?" Nat asked.

"Zombie."

Nat scrunched up his eyes with puzzlement. "Oh, it's what they are though..."

Sin held up his hand and interrupted him. Nat didn't get it—sometimes he wondered if he ever understood Lucy. If he were honest, he didn't get what she ever saw in him. "Don't argue with her. You won't win. I've been trying for a long time now."

Lucy glared at Sin. "I refuse to call them zombies. It's so—stereotypical."

Deyn laughed, amusement filling his eyes. "Oh, then what do you call them?"

"The infected." Lucy shrugged. "It's really what they are. They got infected with a nasty bacteria, and now they are walking corpses."

"Technical. I like it," Deyn said with approval.

"I'm going to give you the injection now. If you experience anything—and I mean *anything*, please let me or Sin know. I need to be aware of any potential side effects."

Deyn nodded. "I know. Can you explain how the vaccine works?"

"It's a complicated process. First, I needed to isolate the antigens needed to create an immune response. This includes gathering the pathogen—or in this case the bacteria causing the disease—and make it inactive." Lucy paused to study Deyn's reaction. She shook her head and started to explain again. "The short answer is I combine them together to create the immune response in your body. It works with your own immunity building cells to fight off the bacteria. You'll have to forgive me if you get me talking technical details I can get carried away."

"I see. So if it works, I'll be immune?" Deyn asked.

"Maybe. I can't guarantee you can't or won't get infected. In a perfect world, you would never get the disease. However, as we don't live in a shiny wonderful Utopia, you could still get it. If it does its job, though, your body should fight off the disease on its own, and you won't become—"

"A walking corpse?"

Sin snickered. "You've converted him, Doll."

Lucy ignored him and asked Deyn, "Are you ready?"

"Yes, inject away."

Lucy scrubbed his shoulder with an alcohol pad and then tossed it on the tray. She uncapped the needle and eased it into his flesh. Deyn flinched as she injected it into him. She pulled the needle out and placed the cap back on it, placing it on the tray.

"There, all done. I will just dispose of the waste in the lab. If you'll excuse me, I need to get back to work. We are on a tight schedule if we are going to leave in three days."

Lucy exited the room not noticing the stunned expressions on Nat and Deyn's faces.

"Three days?" Nat asked. "What is she talking about?"

"I don't trust your intel enough to hang around a week. We need to move to protect her from Wilhelm."

"I see." Nat nodded. "You're right of course. He has too many resources to believe he won't find her again."

"Glad you agree, but I don't really need your approval. Now, I have some things of my own to do. Let me know if you are experiencing any unusual symptoms, Deyn. You can contact me with this communicator."

Sin handed him an ear piece and showed him how to use it. He left the room and didn't look back. There were things he needed to prepare for their upcoming departure. Nat and Deyn could entertain themselves.

6

———

Sin stretched his arms to alleviate the kinks in his muscles. He'd gotten everything ready in a matter of two days. Lucy worked around the clock on her cure. So far the results appeared good, but she still needed more time to get it right. Sin glanced at his watch and decided to check in on her and get a progress update.

He found her doing what appeared to be a happy dance. She bobbled around as her feet slid across the tile floor. Her arms swung around her head in a twirling motion. When she saw him, she ran across the room and threw her arms around his neck as excitement poured out of her.

"Sin, I did it!"

"Did what?" he asked wearily.

"Okay, I think I did it. I believe I found the cure I've been working on forever now." The grin on her face grew to epic proportions. "I'm going to go test it on Nat now."

"Are you sure?"

Her happiness proved to be contagious as a small smile formed on his face, but he had to ask. If she was wrong, it would hurt her a great deal.

"As sure as I'm going to be." She bit her lip. "There's always room for error. I believe this is it."

Good. As long as she realized there was a possibility for miscalculations, they were going to be fine. They could gather their stuff up and leave before her father made an appearance.

"Well then, let's go give Nat and Deyn the good news."

"Let me grab what I need. I'm going to inject him with it now."

Lucy ran to the counter and started putting items in her lab coat pocket. She scooped up a vial filled with a cloudy white liquid and clutched it tight within her grasp. "This right here is the miracle I've been trying to achieve. If it works, I can save a lot of people."

"It'll work, Doll." It had to. Sin didn't want to see any devastation mar her face.

She cupped his face with her free hand. "Thank you for always believing in me. Now let's go see if this miracle actually works."

Lucy wrapped her arm through his and led him out the door. Sin couldn't help the goofy grin growing on his face. Lucy's happiness spread to those around her, and he basked in her light. They walked the entire length of the hall together. When they reached the medical room, they separated. Lucy entered first. Sin following in right behind her.

Nat lay on the bed, face devoid of color. His eyes

dulled to a pale blue—almost the shade of ice—a side effect of the disease running rampant through his body. "Hey, Lucy. Coming to see if I'm still alive?" His attempt at a joke fell flat as dead silence filled the room.

Deyn glared at him with displeasure. "Don't talk like that. You're going to be fine. Lucy will find a cure for you."

"I have to accept reality here. You may not want to believe I'm going to die, but chances are I am going to." Nat turned toward Sin and sneered. "Looks like you might just get your wish."

"Shut up," Lucy shouted. "You're not going to die." Anger tinged her words. "You're such an idiot. Part of me wants to turn around and leave you to your self-misery." She placed her hand on her hips and glared at him. "Lucky for you, I have a conscience and refuse to let you die. If you'd let me speak before you started spouting off that nonsense, you'd realize, I, in fact, may have just found the cure we've all been praying for."

"Really?" Deyn asked. He leaned forward as the beginnings of a smile formed on his face. "You're not making that up are you?"

"Yes. I have it right here." She held out the vial for them to see. Lucy turned to Nat and said, "If you are willing to take a chance, I can inject it now."

"Yes." He nodded. "Do it now. I'm willing to take anything you shove at me if there's a possibility I won't turn into a walking corpse."

"You don't have any questions?" she asked.

Nat shook his head. "No, I trust you. Besides, I'm running out of options."

Lucy took a syringe out of her pocket and plunged

the needle into the vial. She filled it up with the cloudy white liquid and placed the cap over the needle. Sitting on the bed next to Nat she pulled his hand into hers. "Are you ready?"

"Just do it."

She took an alcohol pad out of her pocket and cleansed a patch of skin on his stomach. Without looking where it landed she let the pad drift to the floor as she pulled out the syringe and plunged it into his belly. He grimaced as the liquid entered his system.

"How long until we know if it works?" Deyn asked.

Lucy shrugged. "I'm not sure. An hour, maybe longer. This is all experimental, and Nat is our first test case. I can't predict what is going to happen to him."

"With that piece of good news departed, everyone needs to start packing up essentials. We are leaving tonight," Sin ordered.

"Why so soon? I thought we were not going to leave until tomorrow," Nat said. His eyes a little droopy from exhaustion.

"If Lucy needed the time, we would stay until tomorrow. She's done, so we're getting gone while we know we can. I don't trust Wilhelm to not show up and wreck havoc on our escape."

If it had been up to him, they'd have left when Deyn and Nat showed up. Sin had a bad feeling in the pit of his stomach. It churned as uneasiness settled inside — something horrible was on the horizon. He'd bet on it.

"Where are we going?"

"It's a need to know basis..." Sin paused. "And you don't need to know right now."

"Dickhead," Nat griped.

"Jerkoff." Sin smirked. "As much as I'd like to continue exchanging insults, I really don't have time for it. Start packing. I'll be back in five minutes. Be ready to leave."

"Fine. We will be ready in five minutes," Deyn agreed.

Good, because they were leaving along with them, if they were ready or not. If they didn't get moving, he'd be more than happy to leave them behind. They could deal with Wilhelm all on their own.

"Lucy, come on. We need to pack up your lab. Only take what you absolutely need. Everything else is already at the new facility." Sin grabbed her arm and ushered her out. "I know you'll want to take your grandfather's microscope and your notes on the cure and vaccine. So pack quickly."

They entered the lab in a rush. Sin grabbed a crate and began loading her files into it. She grabbed her microscope and the vials already prepared with the cure and vaccine. Lucy stored them in a cooler with dry ice to protect them while they traveled. They'd practiced this emergency procedure, so they knew how much time they'd have to move on to the next hideout. The only difference was they'd never actually had to use it before —every other time had been a drill.

"Got it all?" Sin asked.

"Yes, let's go."

Sin nodded and picked up his crate. Lucy carried her items, and they exited the lab. They walked down a different hallway to an underground garage. Inside a military grade hummer waited for them. They put their items into the back.

"Wait here. I'll go get Nat and Deyn," Sin said. "Get into the hummer and wait for us. We're going to move out as soon as we're all in the vehicle."

Sin ran down the hallway and into the room where Nat and Deyn were located. They were both standing and waiting for him. "Follow me. We're ready to roll."

They nodded at him and followed him to the vehicle. They got inside and prepared to leave.

"I need you both to arm yourself. There are several guns behind your seats. Choose a weapon and get ready for anything." Sin gestured to his small armory in the back of the hummer.

"Are you expecting a war?" Deyn asked, bewildered.

Sin snorted. Did he expect a response to that? When Deyn raised an eyebrow, it appeared he indeed did. Sin rolled his eyes. "We're already at war. I don't take anything for granted. Wilhelm could be waiting for us even now."

Sin handed Lucy a small compact pistol, one that would fit easily in the palm of her hand, and several magazines.

"What am I going to do with this?" she asked.

"Shoot anyone that gets in our way," Sin replied, deadpan.

"I can't do that," she exclaimed.

"You can and you will," he commanded. "If you don't, it could cost one of us our lives. Do you want to be responsible for that possibility?"

Sin wanted to make things as crystal clear as possible for her. Lucy needed to understand that their lives could very well be in her hands. She couldn't shy away from shooting a gun if necessary.

"I understand," she said in a quiet voice.

"Good." He nodded his head. "Is everyone ready to go?"

"We're all set back here," Nat said.

Sin put the key into the ignition and turned it. The engine roared to life and all the panels lit up in a bright red. He hit a few keys, and a door opened to let them out. Nothing but darkness greeted them. He flicked on the headlights and put the vehicle in drive. Sin punched the gas and exited the compound. As soon as he cleared the doorway, he hit the brakes. In front of him stood hundreds of zombies. All of them clamoring to get to their vehicle.

"Fuck!" Sin swore.

"What are we going to do?" Lucy asked. "There are so many of them. We've never had this many around the compound before..."

Sin scanned the area. Several yards in front of him he spotted Wilhelm. He held a device in his hand. No doubt what he used to control his hoard. They had two choices. Plow through them and hope for the best or back up into the compound and be stuck while he held siege outside their doors. He peeked over at Lucy and dread filled him. He never did tell her about her father's ability to control the infected. Unfortunately, he knew she'd be getting a crash course in their existence in a few short seconds.

"Let me out," Deyn demanded. "I have a few grenades and a rocket launcher I confiscated from your stash. I'll take out a few and clear a path for you."

Nat shook his head. "No, you'll get killed."

"No, I'll be fine." Deyn said, paused, and then continued, "Sometimes a sacrifice needs to be made. I'm willing to do it. Don't argue with me."

"I can't let you. You wouldn't let me, and I'm not going to watch my brother die."

Sin turned to Deyn and nodded his head. He hit the release on the locks, and Deyn hopped out, and rolled across the ground and stopped as his knees hit the ground. A couple grenades already in his hand he pulled the pin and lobbed them into the hoard.

"Damn it. Why did you do that?" Nat asked.

"Because he's right. We're not going to get through without his aid. I have to think of Lucy." She came first —always.

Lucy's face grew white as she watched her father in the distance. A series of loud booms cascaded around them as the grenades started to go off. The zombies swarmed toward Deyn. Sin took advantage and hit the gas. He ran over a few of the zombies to get clear. A little bumpy—but effective—zombies were already dead. Even if they weren't, Sin didn't care. They stood in his way of escape, and Lucy needed to be protected. After he got past the hoard, he let the hummer skid to a halt.

"Nat, I'm going to need you to take over the driving."

"What? why?"

"Lucy knows how to get to the next facility. Make sure you get her there."

"What are you going to do?" Lucy asked.

His face expressionless he turned to her and wanted to lie, but found he couldn't.

"I'm going to end your father's miserable life."

"Don't go, Sin. He's not worth it. I need you," Lucy begged.

Sin shook his head as sadness filled him. He wanted to always be there for her, but Deyn had been right. Sacrifices needed to be made. Nat would make sure she'd be all right. He loved her and realized he'd made a mistake. In time, Lucy, would forgive him. She'd be safe as long as she didn't have to worry about her deranged father.

"You have Nat to take care of you."

Sin hopped out and palmed his hand gun. He rubbed his hand against the pocket of his BDUs to make sure he still had a few extra magazines. Wilhelm watched the zombies as they attacked Deyn. Soon, he'd be out of grenades, and they'd turn their attention on the hummer. Nat better leave soon, or they'd never make it out of danger. Just then, a few zombies jumped Deyn dragging him to the ground as they tore him apart, blood spurted in every direction. Sin cringed and turned his head—he couldn't watch him die. Sin would make sure Deyn's sacrifice had been worth it though.

Sin needed to act fast and kill Wilhelm. The bastard watched with glee as Deyn died. He'd make sure he couldn't ever inflict this kind of damage on anyone again. In complete stealth mode, he moved forward always keeping his eyes on his target. As he neared, Wilhelm turned to him and laughed.

"Ah, Lieutenant Grean. I'd wondered if I'd see you again."

The glee emanating from him put Sin on edge. He was missing something—but what?

"Go to hell, Wilhelm."

"Where's my daughter?"

His agenda was clear, but he wasn't going to get to Lucy. Sin made a promise to her, and he never went back on his promises to his best friend. It was time for her father to die.

"Safe and soon to be completely out of your reach."

God, he hoped so. If Nat still sat there like an idiot in the hummer, he'd fucking murder him. Sin aimed his hand gun, so his shot would hit him square in the forehead.

Wilhelm cackled like a wicked witch—an eerie sound amongst the ensuing chaos. Fuck, the man had insanity shining through his eyes. He was sure more than ever he had something up his sleeve Sin didn't know about.

"Lucy will never be out of my reach again," he said in a sing-song voice. It was so eerie—Sin wasn't easily creeped out and it sent shivers down his spine.

"You're delusional old man. Lucy is long gone."

"Is she?" The man glanced over his shoulder and then turned his evil smirk on Sin. "Somehow, I don't think she is where you left her."

Just as he spoke, Lucy stood behind Wilhelm. One of Wilhelm's soldiers dragged her over to his side. Fuck. Fuck. Fuck. What the hell happened to Nat? Did he make a mistake trusting the bastard? Tears streamed down Lucy's face.

"Let her go," Sin demanded.

"I don't think so." Wilhelm stared at Sin. "I have plans for her. It's time she took her rightful place at my side.

"Father... What have you done?" Lucy stared off into the distance her eyes widened at the horror below them all. "Stop this before you no longer can."

"It's already too late." Wilhelm turned his back to Lucy and faced Sin head on. "Now Lieutenant Grean, what am I going to do with you?"

"Not a damn thing. I'm going to make sure of it." Sin sneered.

"Now, now don't get ahead of yourself. We've only just begun." The man laughed. "Where's the fun in ending it before we've had a chance to begin?"

Sin held his gun steady and watched Lucy out of the corner of his eye. "Just let us go. This can end peacefully." Sin didn't really believe it, but he needed to at least try and reason with the lunatic. At least until Lucy was out of his grasp. After that—Wilhelm was a dead man.

"Father, please listen to Sin. Just let us go. I can't— won't help you..."

"You'll do as I say—if you want your pet over there to live. I can always infect him like your former para- mour...Nat. How is the disloyal bastard anyway?"

Lucy flinched. "You really did infect him on purpose?"

"Did you doubt it?" Wilhelm raised an eyebrow, questioningly.

Lucy drew back and spit. It landed dead center between Wilhelm's eyes. Disgust filled his emerald-green eyes—so like Lucy's and yet completely different. With care, he pulled out a handkerchief from his pocket, wiped his face and glared at her. He stomped over to Lucy's side, drew his arm back and smacked her across the face. Her head whipped back from the force of his blow.

Sin only had a moment to react.

He squeezed the trigger, not letting himself analyze the scene too closely. A bullet whizzed through the air and hit his target. Wilhelm fell to the ground with a loud thud.

Sin turned his gun to the soldier holding Lucy hostage. "Let her go, and I might let you live."

"Might?" he asked.

"I'm still deciding if you're worth allowing the opportunity to live. Anyone working for that bastard deserves to die too."

"You don't know what it's like. He threatened to infect me. Don't kill me. I won't say a word," he begged. "No one is going to care that you ended Wilhelm's life." He held up his hands and backed away from Lucy. "I even know how to deactivate the zombies. If you hit the right button on his device it will kill them all at once."

Sin's gaze went down to the device lying next to Wilhelm. "Lucy pick it up."

Lucy nodded and kneeled before he dead father. She picked up the device and brought it over to Sin. "What do you want me to do?

He had no idea how to work the device. Sin hoped the soldier knew what to do with it because if not—then they'd have a hoard of zombies coming for them soon and no way out. If the bastard lied...he'd be the first one thrown to them as a snack.

"Which button is it?" he asked the soldier.

"The center one. It's the only black button on it."

He kept his gun pointed at the soldier and nodded at

Lucy. "Push the button. If he's telling the truth, we can allow him to live."

Lucy pushed the button and squeezed her eyes shut. As soon as she did, a series of pops could be heard around them. All the zombies' heads exploded from an impact within their brains. They started to fall like dominoes as rows of them fell to the ground.

Awestruck, Sin's mouth fell open as he watched. He shook his head in amazement. "Fuck, that's a sight I'd never thought I'd see."

"Can I open my eyes now?" she asked, her whole body visibly shaking.

"Yes." Sin turned to the soldier. "Run before I change my mind."

The man didn't need to be told twice. He bolted in the opposite direction as fast as his legs could take him. Sin hoped he wouldn't regret letting him live.

"Is it over?" Lucy asked.

"It is, Doll." He held her against him. "I've never been so scared in my life. Where's Nat? What happened?"

"They knocked him out. If nothing got to him, he's probably still there. Hopefully alive. He's still too weak, Sin. Don't be hard on him."

He took her hand within his and moved toward the hummer. Nat still remained slumped over the steering wheel, the door wide open. Sin checked his pulse. He could feel a steady beat beneath his fingers. The gnat still lived. He lifted him out of the driver seat and put him in the back.

"Get in, Lucy. We're going back inside the compound."

"We're not moving on?" Her eyes filled with surprise. "But the compound is compromised—it's not safe."

"No reason to now. With your father dead, we can stay here. Besides, I don't think Nat would make the journey well. You can keep an eye on him and make sure the cure took."

"His color is already better. His fever broke. It's a good sign." She paused and turned her gaze to Sin. "I'm surprised you were willing to leave me in his care without knowing for sure if I'd be safe."

"You were safe. It's why I made sure you had a gun."

"I see," she whispered. "So it's really over?"

"All except for the cleanup. We can let the world know about your cure and the vaccine after you've studied up a little more. Nat can help with it."

"Nat?" she asked. "You're going to trust him?"

"I'll never have faith in him." Sin paused. "But I know you do. You still love him, don't you?"

Lucy sighed. "I don't want too..."

"Don't fight it." Sin smirked. "But don't let that stop you from giving him hell either. Let him earn you back. Trust me, it'll be fun."

It gave something for Sin to anticipate enjoying— perhaps a little too much. It'd be entertaining to watch the gnat squirm a bit. Captain Nathanial Tyger really didn't deserve Lucy, but she made her own choices. Sin just wanted her to be happy.

Lucy shook her head and chuckled as she hopped into the passenger side of the hummer. Sin drove them back inside the compound. It didn't end how he thought it would, but in his mind, it couldn't have gone better. Sure, Deyn could still be alive. No doubt that would have made Nat happy. Sin, however, didn't have any attachments to the guy. He did owe him a bit of gratitude for his sacrifice. So for him, he'd allow the gnat to live and remain a part of Lucy's life.

Read on for an excerpt from Saved by My Blackguard: Linked Across Time 1 AND Broken Pearl

Thank you so much for taking the time to read my book.
Your opinion matters!
Please take a moment to review this book on your favorite review site and share your opinion with fellow readers.

www.authordawnbrower.com

ABOUT DAWN BROWER

USA TODAY Bestselling author, DAWN BROWER writes both historical and contemporary romance. There are always stories inside her head; she just never thought she could make them come to life. That creativity has finally found an outlet.

Growing up, she was the only girl out of six children. She raised two boys as a single mother; there is never a dull moment in her life. Reading books is her favorite hobby, and she loves all genres.

www.authordawnbrower.com
TikTok: @1DawnBrower

BB bookbub.com/authors/dawn-brower
f facebook.com/1DawnBrower
X x.com/1DawnBrower
instagram.com/1DawnBrower
g goodreads.com/dawnbrower

ALSO BY DAWN BROWER

HISTORICAL

Stand alone:

Broken Pearl

A Wallflower's Christmas Kiss

A Gypsy's Christmas Kiss

Marsden Romances

A Flawed Jewel

A Crystal Angel

A Treasured Lily

A Sanguine Gem

A Hidden Ruby

A Discarded Pearl

Marsden Descendants

Rebellious Angel

Tempting An American Princess

How to Kiss a Debutante

Loving an America Spy

Linked Across Time

Saved by My Blackguard

Searching for My Rogue

Seduction of My Rake

Surrendering to My Spy

Spellbound by My Charmer

Stolen by My Knave

Separated from My Love

Scheming with My Duke

Secluded with My Hellion

Secrets of My Beloved

Spying on My Scoundrel

Shocked by My Vixen

Smitten with My Christmas Minx

Vision of Love

Enduring Legacy

The Legacy's Origin

Charming Her Rogue

Ever Beloved

Forever My Earl

Always My Viscount

Infinitely My Marquess

Eternally My Duke

Bluestockings Defying Rogues

When An Earl Turns Wicked

A Lady Hoyden's Secret

One Wicked Kiss

CONTEMPORARY

Stand alone:

Deadly Benevolence

Snowflake Kisses

Kindred Lies

Sparkle City

Diamonds Don't Cry

Hooking a Firefly

Novak Springs

Cowgirl Fever

Dirty Proof

Unbridled Pursuit

Sensual Games

Christmas Temptation

Daring Love

Passion and Lies

Desire and Jealousy

Seduction and Betrayal

Begin Again

There You'll Be

Better as a Memory

Won't Let Go

Heart's Intent

One Heart to Give

Unveiled Hearts

Heart of the Moment

Kiss My Heart Goodbye

Heart in Waiting

Heart Lessons

A Heart Redeemed

Kismet Bay

Once Upon a Christmas

New Year Revelation

All Things Valentine

Luck At First Sight

Endless Summer Days

A Witch's Charm

All Out of Gratitude

Christmas Ever After

YOUNG ADULT FANTASY

Broken Curses

The Enchanted Princess

The Bespelled Knight

The Magical Hunt

EXCERPT: HER ROGUE FOR ONE NIGHT

WICKED WIDOWS' LEAGUE BOOK TWO

DAWN BROWER

PROLOGUE

Claudine Grant glanced up at the dark clouds in the sky. They were an omen of some sort. She had a feeling in her stomach that unsettled her, and had since she'd woken earlier that morning. That feeling of dread wouldn't go away, and as the day progressed it worsened.

Even if the clouds were not an omen of bad things to come they did alert her to one thing with certainty. A storm was brewing. She should go back inside, but she couldn't make her legs move.

She had a letter from her husband, James waiting for her inside. Claudine hadn't opened it yet. Letters from James rarely came. He was away at war fighting against Napoleon. It seemed like an endless war and she feared she would never see him again. What if this was the last letter she ever received from him?

They married one day before he left for war. Their marriage had been quick. Well, as quick as it could be done. The banns were read and after the third week they said their vows. They'd had one night together, and then he had to leave. Then she was alone in their small home. Claudine had two servants—a maid and a cook. James was the third son of a viscount. His commission had given him his rank and position. He was a lieutenant in the Calvary.

All Claudine wanted was for her husband to return to her. She should read his letter. She glanced up at the sky once more and headed home. It didn't take her long to reach the entrance. She went inside and to her writing desk. Claudine pulled out the letter and broke the seal. Folded inside the letter from James was another note. It only had her name scrawled across it. Her hands shook as she picked it up. It wasn't in James' handwriting. Who else would be sending her a letter?

She set it aside and ran her fingers over the words James had written her. His handwriting was so familiar to her. She finished unfolding it and started to read it from the beginning.

My Dearest Claudine,

Today was a good day. There are not to many of those here. The sky was a brilliant blue and the sun bathed us in its light. The warmth felt wonderful against my skin. I wish I could have enjoyed it more. I wish I could have spent this day with you cradled in my arms.

This letter I'm writing out of necessity.

These words should come from me. If the worst should happen... God I can't imagine the worst. Everyone should be able to live their lives with the freedom of not considering that possibility. As a soldier I am not so fortunate. If I had not chosen this life I would be with you.

But if that possibility should happen I don't want to leave anything unsaid. My wonderful, beautiful wife—I adore you. There are no words that can adequately describe how much I love you. The greatest day of my life was when you agreed to be my wife. Our wedding day will be forever honored in my memory. As far as regrets go, that is one thing that will not be tallied under that column. My heart will forever be yours. I will always belong to you, and only you.

My hope is that this letter will be fodder for a fire one day and you will never read it. That soon I'll be home and kissing you, loving you, and spending the rest of my days by your side. However, I must be pragmatic. If you are receiving this letter, then my love, I am no longer amongst the living.

Confirmation will come from someone of authority, but for now, this will have to do.

Before I left I ensured that all my particulars were in order. You will be taken care of, and if you so choose you may remain in the home we selected together. If it doesn't suit you, sell it and find another. And my love...try to let me go. I want you to be happy.

All my love,
James

A tear fell down her cheek. She should have avoided reading the letter longer. She could have remained in blissful ignorance. This couldn't be real. James was not dead. Claudine refused to believe it. She picked up the other folded piece of paper. There was a quick note jotted down there. Almost as if an afterthought…

She needed to read the letter. Claudine's hands shook as she stared down at the parchment. The missive wasn't long. Perhaps that meant it wasn't the news she feared? No. That possibility was unlikely. She had to read it and find out. All the supposition was not helping her.

Dear. Mrs. Grant,

I served with Lieutenant James Grant. He is...was an honorable man. He died in service to his country. You can be proud of the man he was and all that he did. His actions saved the lives of several men in our unit. Without him, there would be more men being mourned. I am sincerely sorry for your loss. Lieutenant Grant will be missed by us all.

Yours truly,
Colonel Andrew Roberts

This letter sounded far more official. She should visit James' father. Perhaps he knew more. She closed her eyes and held back the tears that threatened to fall. Now was not the time for giving in to tears. It was time to plan and get answers.

Claudine glanced out the window. The storm had rolled in. The sky had opened up and rain poured down. It beat against the window like a constant beat of a drum. The roads would be muddy in the morning making them nearly impassible. She would not let that fact stop her. This trip was too important. She'd pack and go to London in the morning. There she would visit the viscount and find the truth. Whatever that truth might be…

Order Here: https://books2read.com/RogueForOne Night

EXCERPT: SAVED BY MY BLACKGUARD

1

———

New York, August 18, 1987

Paul Dewitt tapped his fingers on the arm of the chair. The starkness of the doctor's office was blinding and he couldn't focus on any one thing. The waiting was driving him insane. As the hands on the clock ticked by he could hear parts of his life fall out of existence. What was wrong with him? Why had he passed out? He needed answers and the damned doctor better come and give them to him soon. He wasn't ready to die. There was so much he had yet to accomplish.

The doctor rushed in, sat behind his desk and laid a manila folder on it. He studied Paul with his fingers steepled together in concentration. After a long drawn out silence he sighed and opened the file. He pulled out a sheet of paper and handed it to Paul.

"We've run all the necessary tests and we've come to one conclusion." The doctor paused and stared into Paul's eyes. "You're working yourself to an early grave.

If you don't slow down you won't see your thirtieth birthday."

"What is wrong with me?" Paul glanced at the sheet of paper, but it was all gibberish to him. "Explain what all these numbers mean."

"The short answer is you are too stressed. Your heart is working too hard and you don't sleep enough. Your body is exhausted and fighting itself. It gave in when you wanted to push it past its limits." The doctor grabbed the paper and put it back in the file and closed it. "Despite what you believe, Paul, you're not limitless. You need to take better care of yourself. The best advice I can give you is to take a vacation. Delegate some of your duties and take a step back from your business. From your own admission you work over 80 hours a week. At that pace, you won't live to do anything with the money you're accumulating. Medically speaking, I can only do so much for you."

The good doctor could stick his advice someplace rather unpleasant and twist it like a sharp blade. He couldn't afford a vacation. His company was on the brink of a major takeover of a computer software firm. They held the necessary patents he needed to launch his personal computers on the market. His product would be more affordable to the average family and all the market research showed they would be a high profit margin for his company. Being sick wasn't something he could afford at such a critical time in his family's company. He was the only one who could make sure the takeover went through. His brother was a dismal failure at business and preferred to party rather than taking any responsibility. If he didn't handle everything who would?

"I can't take a vacation." He snorted. "The very idea is ludicrous."

The doctor shrugged. "Ultimately it is your decision. What is more important to you? Your company or your health? I can't make those decisions for you. My job is to point out to you the ramifications of those decisions."

Paul hated to admit the doctor was right. Exhaustion swept through him leaving him drained. He rubbed his eyes, hoping it would help keep him focused. If only he could make it through the next month to see the takeover through… They had to slowly buy up stock using a few different dummy corporations before they could seize control. It would be bad to have the SEC on their backs. He could do some of the work from home if needed. The office and day-to-day business could get by on its own. That was why he had an administrative assistant for. And she was damned good at her job.

"How long?"

"Pardon?" The doctor raised an eyebrow. "How long for what?"

"How long of a vacation do you recommend I take?"

"A month—"

"Is too long," Paul interrupted him. "There's no way I could take a month off from the company. I would end up destitute leaving it for that long."

The doctor shook his head and sighed. "I doubt it would come to that. A week then. Do you think you could manage that?"

Paul tilted his head and considered it. He might be able to manage a week. He could leave detailed instructions with Christy. She knew how he liked things handled and he could depend on her to keep the machine running while he frolicked on the beach. He almost snorted at the absurdity of him lounging on the sand while waves crashed to shore. It wouldn't take him but a day to go mad with boredom. Maybe the doctor was right and he needed to slow down, but to do nothing? That was a fate worse than death. He didn't know how to live a carefree life. It wasn't in his genetic makeup.

"I might be able to take a week, if I have a week to prepare the company for my departure."

The doctor frowned, and then said. "That might be detrimental. Do you need a whole week?"

"Yes," he said, emphatically. "I handle a lot of the details of the company every day. I need time to prepare them for my absence. I know you believe I need this vacation, and you know I disagree. I can't in good conscience leave without doing my due diligence as CEO."

"Fine, but I want you to come by my office in a few days for a stress test. I'm afraid if you push too hard you will have a heart attack before the end of the week."

Was his heart really that overworked? He was tired, but surely the doctor was overreacting. He'd only passed out the once...

"I will have my assistant set up an appointment. I'm not sure when I have a time open."

The doctor nodded. "It really is for the best. When you get back from your vacation I also suggest you cut your work hours by at least a third. Find something else to fill your time with."

"What could I possibly do other than work?" Paul rolled his eyes. "I don't like people and I have no hobbies. Work is all I know."

"I don't know—try dating, find someone to love. Get married, have a family."

Paul almost snorted at his words. He may have been his doctor since he was a small boy, but that didn't mean he had to follow his relationship advice. Women were only good for one thing, and he didn't need one in his life full time to get that. He had no desire to find love. It wasn't in the cards for him and he was all right with that fate. As far as kids, his sister had a couple that could inherit the company. He didn't need any progeny to pass it down to.

"Thanks, but I will have to pass on your sage advice. A family is the last thing I need. You already said I'm stressed, what do you think a wife and kids would do to me?"

"Just slow down. The rest of your life will fall in place once you do. Enjoy your vacation."

Enjoy? Somehow he believed that was the last thing he would do. It didn't matter. If he had to sleep in and be lazy for a week to help heal his heart he would do it. The rest of the doctor's advice wasn't even an option. He didn't need or want someone to nag him for the rest of his life. He was perfectly content the way things were.

"I suppose I can try to anyway. Do you have any recommendations for a vacation spot?"

The doctor shook his head. "No and it doesn't matter as long as you relax wherever it is. You can stay home if you like, just don't go into the office."

"Right." He doubted he would be able to resist the urge to go into the office if he stayed home. So an island getaway it was. He'd have his assistant book his vacation for him. It didn't matter where as long as it was nice and relaxing just as the doctor ordered. "I suppose I will be going. Thanks for the advice."

Paul stood up and left the doctor's office. He had to get back to Dewitt Enterprises and start the plans necessary for his impromptu vacation.

PORT ROYAL, August 28, 1987

The heat of the sun poured over Paul as he lounged on the beach, and the waves crashed on the shore. He pulled his sunglasses off his face and wiped the sweat off his forehead. The forced vacation was already driving him mad.

Sure, Port Royal was amazing and beautiful. There were plenty of stunning sights around him, including the sexy brunette who kept giving him come-hither looks as she strolled down the beach in her tiny white bikini. He couldn't even muster the smallest amount of interest in her—even if she was sexy. The desire wasn't there for him. He'd been on the island two days and he was going stir crazy. He had to do something more than lounge on the beach staring into the sea-green water. At least, he could be thankful he didn't take the doctor's original advice for a month long vacation. That would have been torture he never would have survived through.

Paul sighed. He glanced over his shoulder and an idea took root. There was a lot on this island to see and maybe it was time he started to explore it. The hotel was nice and had every luxury known to man, but he wasn't used to taking advantage of it. His father made sure he understood what was important. The family fortune rested squarely on his shoulders. It was his responsibility to ensure the rest of them lived in the style they'd become accustomed to. The Dewitts came from old money, well as old as an American could come from money anyway. They founded their business early on in the history of the country and managed to hold onto their fortune by sheer will and grit.

If only dad had instilled the same values in his worthless brother and debutante sister.

Paul stood up and headed toward the lush vegetation on the island. A hike along the mountain ridge might be what he needed to loosen up. Sitting around and being lazy didn't suit him, but he could get behind some good old-fashioned exercise. He put his sunglasses back on and started the long trek up the Blue Mountains of Jamaica. He'd meander up a bit, check them out and then head back to the hotel for dinner.

After a short while he stopped at the edge of a cave and looked out at the ocean. It was quite a view. Overhead he saw some cloud formations that had an angry gray appearance. A storm must be heading toward the island. He should head back toward the hotel before he got caught up in a torrential downfall. He started to walk back when he saw a shadow out of the corner of his eye. He turned, startled, as a woman raced ahead of him. Her dress was something from another time. He'd seen enough old pictures to know it wasn't normal to see a woman prancing around in clothing straight out of the eighteenth century. She had long golden blonde hair that fell down her back in waves. Paul was instantly intrigued.

"Wait up, you shouldn't be out here alone. There is a storm coming in."

She ignored him and kept running. The fear in her eyes alarmed him when she glanced over her shoulder. He raced after her as lightning crashed and a thunderous boom followed. Paul had to help her. If he left her alone in the storm he would be the worst cad ever.

"Miss, don't run. I can help you."

Maybe she couldn't hear him. The thunder was rather loud and getting closer with each rumble. The rain began to fall in waves. After a while, he couldn't see two feet in front of him and he'd lost sight of the blonde. He slowly made his way to where he last sighted her. A huge blast of lightning blinded him as a gust of wind blew over him. He scrambled to find his balance, but soon lost it and fell forward. Pain shot through his head and he began to lose consciousness. His arms flailed out as he plummeted toward the bottom of the mountain. His mouth fell open with a silent scream.

So much for being a good samaritan, next time, if he lived through this, he'd leave the woman to her own fate…

2

———

St. Kitts, August 18, 1722

L ady Evelyn Beckett finished dressing in a light muslin gown. The summer heat on the island didn't leave many options for a lady, and she was dying in the sweltering heat. Her long golden blonde curls were drenched with sweat. She sat down and began the tedious process of plaiting them and wrapping them into a tight chignon. Even the smallest loose strand would lead to unwanted warmth on her already over-heated skin.

"Lady Evelyn," a maid said. She curtsied quickly before speaking again. "Pardon my interruption, but your father requests your presence in his study."

Her father, the Earl of Ashland, owned the plantation they currently resided in. She'd lived in England during her formative years, but when her mother died he packed them up and started a new life in the West Indies. Evelyn hated every moment of her time on the island and looked forward to returning to the cooler climate of England. Maybe this was the moment she'd been waiting for. Her betrothed, the Duke of Southington, might have finally summoned her for their wedding.

"Tell him I will be down in a moment." She hid her excitement. It wouldn't do to show her emotions. Her father frowned upon a lady doing anything untoward. "I need to finish my coiffure."

Her father had very strict ideas of what a lady should and should not do. He took being overprotective to extreme lengths. She had a footman, or rather a guard as she thought of the man, who followed her everywhere she went. He denied her a personal maid forcing her to learn how to dress herself properly and see to her own needs. It was supposed to teach her humility. The entire household watched her every move. She couldn't sneeze without someone reporting it to him.

After feeling her hair and glancing over her dress, she was satisfied that she would be presentable and made her way to her father's study. A servant stood outside his door. Evelyn glanced up at him and asked, "Is he available?"

She learned early on not to barge into her father's study. The one and only time she did it her bottom had burned for a week from the whipping he'd given her. It was a mistake she never made again. If there was one thing she did right it was never to repeat the same mistake twice. Living on the island and without a mother's guidance oftentimes left her at a disadvantage—her parents were as different as night and day. Her mother had been loving, kind, and nurturing. She sheltered her from most of her father's darker proclivities. Once she was gone, she saw him for the man he really was. A monster she couldn't wait to escape.

He nodded. "Lord Ashland is expecting you."

She steeled herself to deal with her father and walked stiffly into his study. Gray hair flopped forward, shadowing his face as he bent over his desk and studied a document. She folded her hands in front of her and patiently waited for him to acknowledge her presence and give her leave to sit down. After a few moments he glanced up and gestured her forward. "Evelyn, come in girl. Don't dawdle."

She repressed the urge to roll her eyes. Insolence was forbidden. "Yes, Father."

"Sit. We have much to discuss."

He stood and walked over to a nearby window. The sunlight illuminated him. He was a sturdy man and he'd worked hard to build his fortune in the West Indies. It was starting to take a toll on him. New wrinkles were forming on his forehead and around his eyes every day. Evelyn didn't doubt the stress he put himself under would put him in an early grave. Sadly, she doubted she would miss him once he was gone. He made her life hell.

She sat, waiting for him to tell her why he summoned her. His lack of conversation was making her nervous. Why wouldn't he get it out and tell her what she'd done wrong this time? If it was the duke summoning her for their wedding he'd have already said it. This had to be bad if he left her wallowing in misery.

"I've tried to do my best by you. Raise you right and humble," he began. "I know you must think me evil, but I truly have your best interests at heart."

This wasn't good. He was gearing up to a lecture she wouldn't leave unscathed from.

"Yes, father, I mean no"—she shook her head ardently—"I don't think you're evil." He really was. "I know you only want to make sure I have a good life." As long as she followed his rules and didn't deviate from them in any way.

He laughed. "Don't try and dupe me, girl. I am well aware of what you truly believe." Her father waved a hand dismissively. "It doesn't matter. It's not why I summoned you. I received a letter from the Duke of Southington. It's time for you to return to England for your wedding. It isn't a good time for me to leave the plantation so I'm sending you with a maid as a chaperone. He expects you in England in six weeks for the wedding."

Evelyn gulped. "I understand."

She wanted to jump for joy. Surely the duke would be better than living under her father's care. Six weeks and she'd be the Duchess of Southington, she could hardly wait.

He nodded. "I've already ordered your trunks packed. You're leaving on a ship this evening."

"So soon?" The words were out before she could stop them. She bit her lip and awaited her punishment. It was usually a slap in the face for daring to question him. When no reprimand came, she slowly opened her eyes and was surprised at the expression on her father's face. He looked contrite.

"I've made a lot of mistakes. I won't apologize for them, it's the only way I knew how to raise you. Sometimes I wish…" He shook his head. "It doesn't matter what I wish. If your mother were here she'd be better at this. I'm going to miss you, Evelyn. It's harder to say goodbye than I thought it would be."

This was a side of her father she'd never seen. She had no map to guide her. How was she supposed to respond to this sudden change? If she took a wrong move she could end up regretting it. So she said nothing and waited for him to continue. When there were no adequate words it was better to wait her father out, another lesson she'd learned the hard way. There were too many to count.

"What are you waiting for?" He shooed his hands at her. "Go prepare to leave."

So much for sentimentality, it was nice to see, no matter how brief it was. It showed her that for a small moment in time her father had a heart. He kept it buried too deep for the world to see. In the grand scheme of things it didn't matter. She still wanted to be as far away from him as possible. Surely there was something greater and more meaningful for her life than to be the daughter of an autocratic earl.

So she left him alone in his study, the way he preferred, and went to prepare for her new life.

Out at Sea, August 21, 1722

Evelyn had been aboard the ship for days. For too long they didn't move because there was no wind to guide the sails. The journey was going to take forever at the rate they were traveling. The waves rocked the ship and made her stomach queasy. The daily walks on the deck did nothing to ease her discomfort. Sailing never had been something she enjoyed. The trek from England to St. Kitts had been equally as horrible.

"Lady Evelyn."

Abby's voice broke through her melancholy.

Evelyn turned toward the maid her father assigned to her for her journey and said, "Yes?"

"Perhaps it's time we take shelter in your cabin. Your cheeks are getting red from too much sun."

Evelyn had no desire to be cooped up in her sweltering cabin. She didn't care if her cheeks burned under the sun's heat. It was a blessing to breathe the fresh salt air. She was about to tell Abby that when a shout echoed on the breeze from above.

"Jolly Roger, ahoy!" A sailor called down from the crow's nest.

The first mate scrambled forward, shouting, "All hands hoay!"

Chaos ensued as everyone hurried to get on deck. They forgot about Evelyn in the process and she got shoved against one of the masts. Her head hit it hard and she crumpled to the ground. She stared off into the distance, dazed for several hectic moments.

"Lady Evelyn." Her maid shook her. "You need to get up. Pirates are attacking the ship."

"What?" The words were not registering. "Who is attacking?"

"Have you taken leave of your senses?" Abby shrieked. "Get up now and go to your cabin where you'll be safe."

Abby grabbed her arm and yanked hard. Evelyn barely moved. She shook her head to clear it. What had

Abby said? Oh yes, pirates. The words finally started to penetrate her mind and she got up. Her movements were sluggish and she swayed with each step she took.

"Keep moving," Abby urged.

A blast hit the hull of the ship lurching her forward. Her knees hit the deck hard and took the brunt of her fall. She would have bruises all over her body before this day was done. She scrambled back to her feet feeling her way toward the entrance to get below deck and the safety of her cabin. The cannons fired again and another explosion rocked the hull. Vibrations rolled across her fingers as she moved against the side of the ship.

"Hurry. For the love of God, make haste. We're going to die at this slow pace." Her maid's voice was filled with terror. "Why did I let the earl talk me into joining you on this voyage back to England? I'd be safe in my bed on the island if not for you."

A part of Evelyn knew Abby didn't like her. This was all the confirmation she needed. "If I am such a burden you can leave me alone."

She'd probably be better off without her maid tagging along behind her, spying on her. She didn't doubt Abby would report her every move back to her father. Soon he would have no control over her life. A new man would have that honor. She had only met the duke once when she was a small girl. He'd seemed so foreboding then, but not unkind. Evelyn hoped her original assessment wasn't wrong. It was easy to fool a girl, but as a woman she would see through any façade he presented her. Under her father's tutelage she'd been trained for any possibility. She'd had to grow strong and able to withstand anything because of his unruly temper and exact expectations.

Abby stuck her chin in the air defiantly. "Good riddance too. I'm sure the pirates will find you lovely."

She scooted past Evelyn and headed down to the cabin. It took every bit of strength she had to fight back the tears threatening to fall. Abby had the right of it. Good riddance to her spy and task master. Her life would be inherently easier without having to deal with the maid dictating to her in her father's absence. Maybe the pirates would be a better choice.

"Prepare to be boarded," a pirate called out.

The pounding of feet on the deck filled her ears. Shouts and screams joined the bombardment of noise. Strange men shifted from one side of the ship to the other as they fought for control. The pirates filled the ship and before long they seized power of the vessel. Evelyn wanted to crawl into a hole and seek cover, but the time for hiding had passed.

"What do we have here?"

A husky voice as rich as the Scottish whisky her father preferred filled her ears. Something she shouldn't know much about, but out of curiosity she'd sneaked a taste or two of the amber liquor. Evelyn looked up and stared straight into eyes the exact shade of the Caribbean Sea. The pirate's golden-blond hair shimmered in the sunlight. He was perhaps one of the most beautiful men she'd ever gazed upon. She'd heard pirates were a dirty lot, but this one was surely a different breed altogether.

"Who are you?"

He studied her for a moment and then his lips tilted into a wicked smile. It made him intrinsically more appealing. The sexy beast was too gorgeous for his own good. He would be devastating to the female population if he were unleashed upon them.

"Captain Jack Morgan at your service." He bowed to her. "Percy, come help the Lady board the Siren Song. She's going to join our crew as my mistress."

"But Capt…" The pirate stammered.

"Are you refusing to follow a direct order?" Captain Morgan glared at him.

"No, Captain." He bowed his head in submission. He leaned in and said with a loud whisper, "Women are a curse on board a ship."

"I don't bow down to superstition. This woman is mine and I intend to keep her." The captain waved a hand dismissing the other pirate. "Now, do what I ordered."

Evelyn turned her head back and forth between the two. Did the pirate captain say she was going to be his mistress? Over her dead body… She was meant to be a duchess and she'd be damned if she let that man lay a hand on her. He might be astoundingly striking, but her father hadn't raised a fool.

"I am no man's mistress," she spat out, finally finding her voice, and the spine she'd grown dealing with her father's tyranny.

"Of course not, you're Captain Morgan's and he's no mere man."

Evelyn's gaze flew toward the pirate who'd cowed before his captain. "I don't recognize him as someone in need of worship. He might be a god to you, but he's nothing to me."

Captain Morgan laughed. "Let her be for now. She'll come around in time. They all do."

A cocky smile filled his dazzling visage. Evelyn wanted to wipe it permanently off his face. He was so damned sure of himself. How many women had fallen at his feet? She would not be among them. "You can wait till the end of time. I will not be changing my mind."

"We'll see, love." His grin widened and he traced her jaw with the tip of his finger. "I've been told I have a magic touch."

She shivered involuntarily. Why did he have to be so bloody handsome? "I wouldn't know. You do nothing for me."

He chuckled lightly. "I like this one. She has spirit. We're going to have a lot of fun together." He turned toward the other pirate. "Take her aboard the ship now." He gestured his arms toward the ship Evelyn had been sailing on before they attacked. "As for this one, scuttle it."

Percy yanked her toward the gangway and hauled her across it toward their ship.

"What did the captain mean by scuttle it?"

"He means to sink the ship." Percy didn't even bother to look at her. He kept pulling her toward a cabin on the ship. He shoved her inside and locked it from the outside.

"You can't murder everyone on the ship." She banged on the door.

The last thing she thought she heard him say was, "Not your call to make."

Then there was nothing but silence, leaving Evelyn alone with her own dreary thoughts. There was no saving her from the fate she found herself in. She had only herself to rely on. Jack Morgan believed she'd willingly fall into his arms. He didn't know her or her resolve. As long as he didn't force her she could withstand his advances. She took a deep breath and forced herself to relax. She would need her strength for the upcoming battle.

www.ingramcontent.com/pod-product-compliance
Lightning Source LLC
Chambersburg PA
CBHW051856130726
47987CB00002B/864